The Little Bayou Fairy

Written and Illustrated by Erica Ramsey-Bowen

Dedication

For My Truly Amazing Goddaughter Marissa,

The 185 Wonderful Kickstarter Supporters of This Book,

All the Trusting and Patient Advance Readers,

and YOU...

I Love You All and Promise to Remember:

Behind

Every Successful, Happy

Little Fairy

Is

Exceptional

Village

Encouragement

An Illustrated Map of the Little Bayou Fairy's Journey:

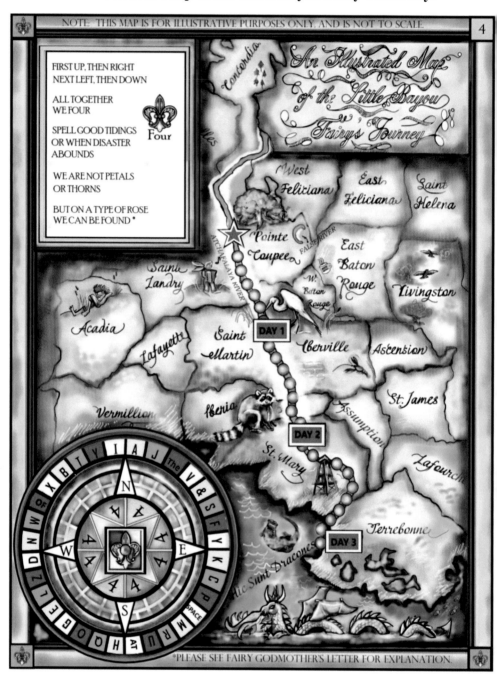

Table of Contents

KICKSTARTER SUPPORTERS:

Bumblebees:
Adam P. Minott
Angela Marshall
Emily Huneycutt
Gloria Irigoyen-Salinas
Kate Farrow
Meryl McLaurin
Trudy Porche
Yvonne Fisher

Baby Chick:
Anne Hunter
Beth North
Brad and Cynthia Mitchell
Cindy Cox
Cindy Treadaway
Deborah Cornwell
Dawn Duhon
Dee Davis
Ilana Joffe
Katherine Bynum
Leona Eubanks
Lisa Baermann
Luis O Gutierrez
Kathleen McCarthy
Marianne Ciovacco Reddick
Mary Kluth
Michelle Widebeck Sharp
Nancy Dworek
Sandra Holbrook
Sarah Bolen
Susan Warren
Susan Ze
Suzanne Ladd
Theresa Hayes

Big Chick:
Amber Miller
Becki Fisher
Brina Daniels
Carla Foley
Debbie Karimullah
Ellen McCaulley
Gail Donkers
Ginger Kilbreth
Jessica Manfredi Carter
Julie Dwyer
Julie Nickel
Karen Hynninen
Kathleen Dorgan
Mary Ann Weigand
Mil Ivey
Millicent Coleman
Penny Hollis Stark
Sharon Byrd
Stephen Urbrock
Vicki Cocks

Barn Owl:
Adria Negelow
Alexis Horlbeck Sipmann
Allison Milligan
Ben Needle
Candy Williams
Carla Jukes
Courtney Daly
Deborah White
Edie Nugent
Gina Therayil
Jack and Amy Kelly
Jennifer Rhorer
Julie Layland
Karen Woolford
Kristel Calvert
Laura Wilson
Patrick Flaherty
Regine Sawyer

Blue Butterfly:
Alexis Molnar
Alicia Urquhart
Ahsan Rahim
Cheryl Godwin
David Arnold
Dawn and Rudy Garza
Delphine LaGroon
Doug Harmon
Heather Maddox
Hugh Carter
Hynden Walch
Jamie Thompson
Jennifer Tyree
Josh Welch
Kalila King
Karen DeRuyter
Kelli Fridge
Kelly Hannum
Kenn Walker
Kristin Lloyd Moussa
Kristina Avera
Leena N' Jim
Linnea Thurston
Mannie Pallia
Melanie Woodard
Monique Hudson
Nadine Deschene
Pamela Freeman Cavin
Penelope Fuller
Renee and Jon Hobbs
Sandra Huss
Stephen Franzese
Teresa Hildebrand
Theresa Brightwell
Tyra Paytes
Wade Patrick

Ladybug Library:
Charles A Ramsey II
Doug Wise
Gretchen Patrick
Leslie "Chef Mo" Porche-Smith

River Turtle:
Angelique Roche
Beth Volden
Brian Monette
Deryl Alexander
Jason and Shelby Behret
Karen Jones
Kathi Goodwin
Leslie Clark
Lindsay Prose
Megan Rae Collins
Rick Davis
Robert and Cheryl Leydon
Roderick
Tyler Peabody
Wendy Walker

Chipmunk:
Carl H. Walker
Kathi Goodwin
Leslie Crowder

Silver Fairy:
Dr. Keith Ramsey, MD

The St. Augustine "Jolly Seniors" & Their Families:

Gracie Armstrong
Geneva Ashford
Gerry Battley
Clara Burks
Joyce Butler
Hilliard Caldwell
Barbara Carter

Pamela Christophe
Jasmine Christophe
Jeremiah Christophe
Kohen Christophe
Lois Christophe
Mary B. Derosin
Mildred Duhe

Soror Val Dukes/Amari Hills
Gloria Facione
Marynette George
Beverly Hurst
Wylene Hurst
Louella Johnson
D'Andre M. Joseph

Dorothy C. Joseph
Onora Kimble
George LaCour
Gura J. LaCour
Joseph B. LaCour
Mary Lou LaCour
Elayne Ladmirault

Theresa Lee
Louise Martin
Mary Norwood
Crystal Polar and The Boys C&C
Nora Porche
Glynette Shepherd
Sophia Thomas

With Deep and Humble Appreciation:

These pages are dedicated to my wise Volunteer Fairy Council and Kickstarter Supporters in appreciation
of their support, love, and financial backing!
Without You, *The Little Bayou Fairy* would never have found her True North.
I Love You All and Thank You From the Bottom of My Heart!

The Little Bayou Fairy Volunteers Aka the Wise Fairy Council "Brain Trust":

Lisa Bagley (Lisa "BEE")
Letitia Martin Bajoie
Shelby & Jason Behret
Theresa Kelly Brightwell
Kristel Calvert
Leslie Blackmon-Clark & Kicker Diva!
Millicent Glover Coleman
Megan Rae Collins
Leslie Crowder
Rhonda Ebron Davis & Her Littles ☺
Nadine Deschene
Tasha Dillsaver
Jeff Frank
Larae Lewis Johnson & Family
Tawanda Johnson & Family
Kelly (and Klara!) Hannum YOU ROCK
Amy Kelly and Jack Kelly
Kim Long Kramer
Delphine LaGroon
Dan "The Man" Lanihan
Lisa V. Moore
Kristin Lloyd Moussa
Tyra Sias Paytes
Tyler, Daniel, and Lilith Peabody
Lissette Perry
Leslie "Chef Mo" Porche-Smith
Tandria and Trayvon Potts
Debra Arceneaux Ramsey
Gina Taylor Tharayil
Royce Tribue
Deborah White
Melanie Arceneaux Woodard
Carla Wright-Jukes
Jessica Manfriedi Carter

In Memoriam:

Special Shout Outs to The Following Supportive Organizations And Mentors:

All of my Godparents who may have inspired a certain character in this tale:
Charles and Stella Gremillion, Norma and Paul Duell (Rest In Power), Kay and
Ron Patterson
All of the Tiny Humans and Their Parents Who Helped Me Lighten Up and
Become A Kid Again During My Online "CAMP CORONA" – You Guys Are Stars
All of my Author Friends Who Understood About Breakdowns and My
Pandemic Creative Brain Pain – I Love Each and Every One of YOU!
Al Donato and Natalie Stechyson of the Huffington Post Canada
Allison Giddens
Boomer the WonderDog, Chloe E. Cats and the now defunct Orange Cat Mafia
Mrs. Dianne Gaines
False River Rotary Club
Holy Cross Catholic Church, Durham, North Carolina
John Ray of North Fulton Business RadioX
Lisa Ferland and Lisa Ferland Consulting
Louisiana Tri-Parish Delta Sigma Theta
My amazing supportive family and friends of OUT Georgia Business Alliance
Peggy Morrow
Rick Davis
Rivka, Andrew, Shoshanna and Miss Naomi
Shelley and Tom Negelow & Adria and Josh Saul
Sara Troy of "An Author's Kiss"
Jeannie and the entire West Baton Rouge Museum Staff
Dean Wilson and Monica Fisher of Atchafalaya Basinkeeper
Steve Franzese
The Atlanta Budokan
The Rotary Club of East Cobb
The Multitude of Magical and Gifted "BEE-ans" of Lisa Bee's Facebook Tribe
My ever-patient, long-suffering, glitter-encrusted husband, Scott
My mother, who endured years of my endlessly spinning yarns to and from
school, listening with the saintly patience only a mother could have. And when
her patience ran out, had the foresight to have Chee-tos in the car!
And last but never least - to my Creator, the Ultimate Artist, Author, and Editor
of us all – thank you for this life and endless inspiring treasure of color, beauty,
laughter, beguiling fairy tales, glittery unicorn poop, and that most magical of
all words - hope.

I began to type the names of all the souls lost that I knew of during the pandemic, but then realized we all lost so
many and so much. It was a depressing exercise... so I decided to drop that and instead remind you (me) that
sometimes the bravest thing one can ever do in life is to just show up and keep putting one uncertain foot in front
of the other. Namaste.

Chapter One:
The Little Bayou Fairy

Once upon a time, there was a Little Fairy. She was not like an elegant fairy you perhaps have read about in books. She was not willowy with large, colorful butterfly-like wings, and she did not glow brightly like other fairies, in hues of vivid purple or bright pink or lustrous green or sparkling blue.

Instead, she was brown, small, and round. She had furry, brown moth-like wings that barely carried her through the air. And instead of glowing an intense colorful light like the other fairies, she emitted a very faint, dim golden yellow hue, like a far-away star.

This Little Fairy and her family of fairies lived in a lush wild watery area called a *bayou* within the Atchafalaya Basin in Louisiana a long time ago, when things like seeing fairies in your backyard were quite ordinary.

The Little Fairy caused her Mother and *Grand-Mère* (grandmother) much distress. She was so strange and different from the other fairies. And the other fairy children were quick to make her feel even smaller and stranger than she already was.

Every day after flight school and dance class, the Little Fairy would usually fly home in tears. The other fairy children made fun of her dull-colored odd little wings, her near-sightedness, her unusually small size, her roundness, and her extreme clumsiness.

"Bumble bee! Bumble bee!" they laughed, as she fumbled and tumbled about unevenly in the air during flight school.

"Hey FUMBLE bee! Pick a lane!" they taunted as she crashed into the ground during dance class.

"HI bumble bee! BYE bumble bee!" they'd giggle and whisper to one another. She was always last to the finish line of any aerial race. Every single one of them would pass her in the air.

Her Mother encouraged her to drink more flower nectar, practice her flying, and learn to dance more gracefully among the flowers on the *levee*.

"If you want the other fairy children to stop making fun of you, you need to fit in more, do the things other fairies do," her Mother told her.

"But flower nectar makes me jumpy and fidgety," the Little Fairy said. "And I get queasy when I fly. Everything looks swimmy, I get headaches, and feel like passing out. And I can NOT dance. My feet get crisscrossed, and I end up crashing into the other fairies. And my toes hurt in those fancy fairy dance shoes."

"But what do you like to do, then?" her Mother asked.

"I like swimming and playing with the fish," she said.

"*Alors!*" said her Grand-Mère, peering at the Little Fairy through magnifying eyeglasses mounted on the end of a wand, called a *lorgnette*.

She held her lorgnette close to her face and ogled the Little Fairy, "No grandchild of mine has *ever* swum!"

"*Alors!*" moaned her Mother. "My child, play with the fish? I think not!"

"We are not common brownies or irresponsible water sprites. We're supposed to fly about and dance. We're fairies." lectured Grand-Mère.

"Then maybe I'm a… changeling?" said the Little Fairy, looking down at her feet.

"A WHAT?" Her Mother gawked. "How do you even know such a word???"

The Little Fairy felt like she had committed a major offense. "Sometimes… the other fairies make fun of me and call me that."

"Well!" huffed her mother. "That is – well that is just… ridiculous!" And she crossed her arms and turned about slowly in the air, something she did when particularly distressed.

"But what about the legend of Silka the Swan? She was born a duck or at least they thought she was a duck-,"

"Silka was NOT a duck changeling– it's a known matter of fact that swans are always careless with their eggs!" Her Mother shook her head, resolutely. "They're beautiful and graceful but those silly creatures have not much more than fluff for brains. For heavens sake, *I* almost hatched a baby swan myself once from a random egg that rolled into my boudoir!"

"But what about Christophe the *fifolet* who was in love with the North Star? Legend has it that one night he turned into a blue glowing vapor-,"

"Hmph! A nonsensical fairy tale told to scare fairy babies and keep them from flying off into the cane fields alone!" her Grand Mère said, her lips pursed tight. "You must stop entertaining these wild fancies and face facts. **YOU** ARE A FAIRY! **WE** are **ALL FAIRIES**. There are no such things as changelings! And you should be proud of your lineage! Our family hails from a long line of great fairies. You must learn to be a proper fairy and stop doing these crazy things!"

"You must practice! Practice! Practice!"

"But flying is too hard!" groaned the Little Fairy. "I can barely stay aloft and I'm always bumping into things or falling into

12

things or falling ON someone or something! Why can't I play with the fish? What's wrong with that? I *like* the fish. They tell me amazing stories about the seas, rivers, and strange creatures that live under the water."

"Flying would NOT be so hard if you practiced every day with discipline and diligence, like Sakura and Aster," her Mother said.

The Little Fairy's older twin sisters, Sakura and Aster, were indeed excellent fairies.

Sakura and Aster

Sakura was noted for creating never-before-seen aerial acrobatics in her flight choreography. Her twin sister Aster was renowned throughout the land for her sense of style and her ability to design fabulous outfits. And no fairy in all of Louisiana could compare to either sister when it came to dancing.

Even so, the twins were not content with being merely great at their craft, but tirelessly practiced every single day at becoming even better.

"*That's* how one becomes a proper fairy," her Grand-Mère added, gesturing with her lorgnette towards the Little Fairy's sisters. They were outside as usual, rehearsing what appeared to be an overly complicated dance.

Grand-Mère waved her lorgnette like a baton for emphasis. "You must *practice! Practice! Practice!*"

This made the Little Fairy sad.

She practiced all the time and really was doing her best to be a proper fairy, but none of the things the other fairies did ever made sense to her.

She simply wasn't good at doing any proper fairy things.

CHAPTER TWO

MONSIEUR BON CHANCE

Chapter Two:
Monsieur Bon Chance

The wisest creature in the Atchafalaya Basin where the Little Fairy lived was a large blue-gray catfish with long whiskers who everyone called Monsieur Bon Chance. *Monsieur*, in case you did not know, is French Creole for "mister," and the expression *bon chance* means "good luck". The catfish was too old and too wise for any mere human to catch him. So, the Creoles named him 'Monsieur Bon Chance' after many frustrated, and fruitless, attempts to catch him for supper.

Oftentimes, he would pretend like he was caught, wriggling and thrashing and yanking the fishing lines like he was desperate for escape. Then, once he tired of the game and the fishermen were exhausted from his antics, he would escape by spitting out their fishhooks, tangling their lines, and swimming away, his jowls and belly full of the tasty bait.

The Little Fairy and Monsieur were good friends. Once, the Little Fairy had helped Monsieur avoid a nasty fishing net that had been laid to ensnare him. Even though Monsieur probably would have escaped the net, as he always had, he admired the Little Fairy for being so kind and sweet in nature.

So it was that he that told her of the waters beyond the bayou, where the streams led into the rivers, which then led into the sea.

None of the fairies had ever seen the sea. They were all bayou-bound creatures and thought the Atchafalaya was the only sensible place for fairies to live.

Live in the open in salty air with no sweet flowers to drink nectar from? "Horrors! *Alors!*" they would have exclaimed at the very idea of something so absurd.

Swim in the deep blue seawater among creatures the size of the levees? "Why?" they would have shouted. "Those gigantic creatures would eat a tiny fairy! *Sacré bleu!*"

But the Little Fairy listened eagerly to the descriptions of the changing tides, the sand dunes, and sea oats. Most of all, she loved to hear of the playful dolphins, ghostly jellyfish, and enormous, stately whales.

It all sounded so mysterious and delightful to her.

"I myself have never seen these things," admitted Monsieur Bon Chance, blowing a few round bubbles from his gaping mouth. "But I know they exist. If I were to leave my comfortable, warm bayou and swim south for three days hence, I would reach the sea, yes, *la mer*, with her glittering crown of water and her riches of seashells and shining sand. But I am an old fish, and it satisfies me to play simple tricks on these Creoles and Cajuns and cause a ruckus. So, here I am, and here I remain. *C'est ainsi.*"

"But *I* am not old, Monsieur" piped up the Little Fairy.

The wise old fish regarded the Little Fairy. "No, indeed, you are not," he said slowly. He was clearly thinking interesting thoughts. "Your life is ahead of you—ready, open, waiting for adventure, yes?"

"Yes!" said the Little Fairy. "I'd love to go on an adventure and see the ocean and all the things you have described. And maybe just --- find a place where I fit in. None of the other fairy children here even like me. They call me... bumblebee." Her chin quivered as she whispered the dreaded word.

"Ah, they do? They call you a bumblebee? *Mais, que formidable!*" (That means 'But how wonderful!')" said Monsieur Bon Chance, cheerfully.

"Wonderful– what? No – being called 'bumblebee' is *not wonderful*. In fact, that's the absolute *worst* thing you can call a fairy!" huffed the Little Fairy.

"Ah, so?" asked the Monsieur. "Then these little fairies do not know the miracle of the bumblebee. What a shame. You see, I will tell you a secret."

And Monsieur leaned in, whispering conspiratorially, his gleaming whiskers waving to and fro in the warm water's current.

"Little one, did you know a bumblebee is really not supposed to be able to fly? For many years, people have been - how does one say it - *fit to be tied*? Trying to figure out how can this be? How can the bumblebee fly? The bumblebee's wings – they are small, you see – a little like yours – and their bodies a little round and not at all light – erm, also something like yours. But they fly anyway! Because no one has ever told them they could not! So you see, these silly little fairy children that make fun in calling you 'bumblebee'– they are in fact, really complimenting you. They are actually calling you *a miracle*."

Monsieur was silent for a few moments and blew a few round bubbles while the Little Fairy considered this.

Finally, he interrupted her thoughts "*Ma petite fee* (which means 'my little fairy') . . . the day grows late, and I have no more time to talk about miracles and adventures today. I think I spy a fisherman I know, and he is using my favorite bait—pink marshmallows! That would make a most satisfying supper."

21

Monsieur Bon Chance chuckled, his eyes gleaming with mischief, enjoying the idea of giving the fisherman a run for their money.

"We can speak more later of *la mer*, yes, my good Little Fairy? And so, *adieu!*"

Then, with a dramatic *swish swish,* and a *plop,* he disappeared beneath the water.

The Little Fairy stared at the tiny trail of bubbles left in his wake.

She then flew slowly home (flying very close to the ground with her eyes almost closed to keep from getting sick). Monsieur's encouraging words gave her a lot of new ideas to consider.

Had she stuck around, just a few moments later, she would have heard the frustrated screams of a fisherman in his pirogue cursing the clever Monsieur Bon Chance. Monsieur had once again tangled the fishing lines and stolen the prized bait of fluffy pink marshmallows.

CHAPTER THREE

POLONIUM - OXYGEN

PHOSPHORUS + IODINE + HYDROGEN

INDIUM · NITROGEN + RADIUM

13

+ TELLURIUM + SULFUR +

THE FAIRY GODMOTHER

Chapter Three:
The Fairy Godmother

Later that evening, in the twilight, all of the bayou fairies were doing what they loved most: dancing and performing aerial tricks among the limbs of the biggest oak tree that grew alongside the levee.

That particular oak tree had many large limbs that curled down and around like large ribbons made of wood. The oak limbs made perfect runways for the fairies to land and take off and the tree's long elegant drapes of Spanish moss framed multiple stages that showcased the fairies dancing, twirling, and leaping into the air. The entire scene was something to behold.

If you have ever seen fireflies on a purple summer evening, then you have an inkling of what fairies dancing around that oak tree would look like – except the dots of light were moving much faster and instead of just yellow dots, there were hundreds of all different colors of dots, winking and darting about. That is how fairies look when dancing and it is an amazing thing!

That particular evening, all of the fairies were having a magnificent time – except one.

And I bet you can guess precisely who that one was.

It was, of course, the Little Fairy.

Who, of course, felt quite miserable, uncomfortable, and entirely out of place.

She hid from the fairies' wild exuberant dancing and merry-making and tried her hardest to not be noticed by cowering silently on the ground within the darkest nook of the oak tree's vast trunk, behind a clump of wilted dandelions.

Of course, by sitting quietly and hiding on the ground, rather than flying and dancing, she only stood out even more. She did not even touch the leaf cup of nectar by her side. Everyone noticed, including her Mother and Grand-Mère. They were both so ashamed, they pretended not to see her. And their shame and pretense made her feel even worse. She felt she just couldn't do anything right.

Have you ever felt that way, dear reader?

If so, then you know what a terrible, sad, hurtful feeling it can be. And as she felt this way, the Little Fairy's faint golden light that usually emanated brightly from within her, seemed to dim and flicker, like a flame on a candle, struggling to stay lit.

Throughout the evening, Sakura and Aster would occasionally fly to their sister's side to check on her, try to cheer her up, and coax her into joining the dance. But each time their little sister would sadly shake her head at them and retreat even further into her dark hiding spot.

I think this is a good place to stop for a second and explain a few pieces of fairy etiquette. *

Not dancing when you happen to be a fairy is like sneezing without covering your nose and not even bothering to say "pardon me".

It is considered quite rude among fairies.

And not flying when you are a fairy is even more rude... it is like belching especially long and loud at a formal dinner where people are all dressed up and about to make a fancy toast or something.

And not drinking perfectly good NECTAR when you are a fairy... well, I will just leave that to your imagination as to what *that* means. I think you get my meaning.

28

"Little one, why are you not dancing? And why are you not flying? And why is your flower nectar cup untouched?"

The Little Fairy (who had her head down all this time, so that she wouldn't get dizzy from the lights of the other fairies zig-zagging about in the air) raised her head.

Before her, hovering a bit in the air was a beautiful, sparkling, fairy with shiny silver hair, glowing deep brown skin the hue of a perfect pecan, fluttering in the air with the most delicately translucent set of silvery wings and wearing a shiny, shimmery dress decorated with many, many teeny pockets. The light she gave off was a bright shining silver. It made the Little Fairy gasp just to behold her.

The Little Fairy felt like she knew this fairy. She seemed familiar and yet the Little Fairy had never seen such a creature at any of the fairy dances before.

But her face and voice were kind, so the Little Fairy had the courage to tell her the truth.

"I'm not flying and dancing because I don't fly very well and I don't like dancing," she gulped. "My feet get all twisty."

"Ah," said the Silver Fairy.

"And when I DO try any kind of somersault, my stomach aches, I always end up crashing, and my head hurts when I go too fast."

"I see," said the Silver Fairy.

Author's Note: See compendium excerpt in the back sharing a portion of the fairy etiquette manual by that famed grand dame of fairy correctness, Madame Daisy Nettlebee of the Baton Rouge Nettlebees.

"And nectar, in my opinion, is kind of... over sweet. It makes me feel jumpy and jittery," she said.

"Um-hum, I think I understand," nodded the Silver Fairy.

"You do?" asked the Little Fairy.

The Silver Fairy nodded. "I do."

The Silver Fairy touched the Little Fairy's forehead. It was a simple thing, but when she did so, the Little Fairy felt a huge relief, like a stone had been lifted off her heart.

"I understand and I know how you are feeling... because I am your Fairy God Mother. Some fairies are lucky enough to have Fairy God Mothers, not all, but some. So, *you* must be *extraordinarily lucky* because I am yours."

"*I'm* lucky? I mean – I've never heard of you before. And no one I have ever known has a Fairy God Mother. What is it exactly that Fairy God Mothers *do*?" asked the Little Fairy, shyly.

The Silver Fairy sighed and smiled. "We listen," she said simply. "We listen to our little Godchildren without expecting that they do this or do that or say this or say that. And we always watch from afar, just to see if we should perhaps lend a listening ear during uncertain times."

"You just – listen?" the Little Fairy squinted.

The Silver Fairy wrinkled her nose and winked.

"Well, that's pretty much the biggest part of what we do. I know. It sounds like a silly thing but it's actually quite hard. It's truly a magical trait. Have you ever tried to listen to someone, I mean *really listen*, without interrupting?"

The Little Fairy's mouth made a perfect wondering O shape. She had tried listening like that before. And it was indeed nearly impossible.

"And so now you know that I am here to listen to you." And the Fairy Godmother smiled so wide, her whole face was a beaming crescent and the Little Fairy felt strangely like she had been given a most precious gift.

"So, Little Fairy, you seem to have a good idea about what you *don't* like to do... what is it you *do* like to do?"

The Little Fairy thought for a moment.

"Hmmm," she said, finally. "I like to swim. I like to talk to fish, and oh, I haven't seen it, but I know I would just *love* the ocean! I might want to even live there it sounds so perfect. Did you know there are beings there called *'seahorses'* but they don't have legs like the ones here and they never walk on land? And did you know there are things in the ocean called *'whales'*? And that they are almost the size of levees? And their babies are called *'calves'* just like baby cows are called calves here? And did you know-?"

The Little Fairy's Godmother suddenly laughed, and the Little Fairy stopped speaking at the sound.

Then she realized her Fairy Godmother's laugh was kind. It was a soft, warm sound, not at all like she was making fun, but as if what the Little Fairy said had delighted her deeply.

"I did not know any of that. But it all sounds very interesting, and you certainly are very *very* excited about it all. You want to be a fairy who lives by the ocean... an ocean fairy... hmmm... now that's something new under the sun. Have you told your family about any of this?"

The Little Fairy looked up sadly at her Mother and her Grand-Mère, who were busy dancing, merrily flitting about, and laughing in the twilight along with the other fairies. Then she looked over at her two sisters who had just finished a complicated aerial display featuring backwards loop-de-loops. They were being applauded madly by their admiring audience and entreating cries of *"Encore! Encore!"* resounded from all around.

"No. I've tried and tried to tell them. They don't listen to me," the Little Fairy said softly.

Her Fairy Godmother nodded, pursing her lips.

"I see what you mean. Well, it is obvious what you like and what they like are not the same. So, there is only one thing to do," she said.

The Little Fairy looked up at her Fairy Godmother.

"And what is that, Godmother?" the Little Fairy asked.

Her Godmother bowed her head and began rummaging through the many teeny pockets on the front of her shimmering dress. Suddenly, she stopped, exclaimed, "Ah HAH!" and pulled a silvery something out of one.

The Little Fairy next realized the "something" her Fairy Godmother took from her pocket was a necklace. Without even pausing, her Fairy Godmother reached down, and placed the necklace over the Little Fairy's head and made sure it was fastened securely around her neck.

"There is a place for **EVERYONE** in this big wide wobbly world, including a place and a tribe somewhere out there - intended just for you," she said softly, just loud enough for only the Little Fairy's ears to hear. "That's why our Creator made our beautiful world so very big."

She paused while the Little Fairy considered this.

"And since you feel so strongly that you have no place here where you belong, you must be brave, tell your family honestly what you desire, and then... go out into the world yourself and *find it*," she whispered.

The Little Fairy thought about that and looked down at the necklace. An odd silverish stone hung on it, with some sort of blue and silver figure carved upon it. When she looked at the figure, it seemed to move and swim around and around the stone, making figure eights and squiggles across its surface.

"But," she began to speak, looking up.

There was no point in finishing what she was going to say.

Her Fairy Godmother had vanished in those few short seconds, evaporating into the air with a mysterious smile and wave of farewell. And as her Godmother's disappearing hand waved farewell, a shower of bright, silvery, glittery sparkles fell around and onto the Little Fairy, and then they too disappeared, like melted stardust.

"Fairy Godmother! Fairy Godmother! Wait!" the Little Fairy called out anxiously, jumping to her feet with a panicked flutter of her wings.

"You'll see me again," the Little Fairy could hear her Fairy Godmother's voice calmly reassuring her, even though she was no longer visible. And as her Fairy Godmother's voice continued to speak, it grew softer with each word as if she were talking from a place that was farther and farther away by the second.

"Goodbye! God bless you, Little Fairy!" Her Fairy Godmother 's voice said, even more faintly.

"And remember my little ocean-seeking adventurer:

BE BRAVE!"

CHAPTER FOUR

HER JOURNEY BEGINS

Chapter Four:
Her Journey Begins

"YOUR CONDUCT TONIGHT AT THE DANCE! What WERE you THINKING?" The Little Fairy's Mother was yelling once they had all arrived at their cozy leaf home later that evening.

Her Grand-Mère burst into noisy tears and pressed her tiny lace handkerchief to her face.

This made the Little Fairy's Mother even more upset.

"Your poor Grand-Mère and I had to listen to all of the other fairies whispering that you had gone mad... that you spent too much time speaking with that slippery, bubble-blowing- water-rat-of-a-rascal, Monsieur Bon Chance! And... AND! That... that you... would end up like your eccentric Auntie Bluebell and... and...," her voice quavered, and she whispered, horrified, "*marry a troll and live in a slimy grotto!*"

The very idea shocked everyone into a sudden silence.

"Oh, but no! A granddaughter of *mine,* marry a *troll* and live in a *grotto*? *Mais non!*" gasped the Little Fairy's Grand-Mère, now fanning herself with her handkerchief, her eyes wide with the thought of such a disgrace.

"I'm so sorry," said the Little Fairy. She wanted to hang her head, but she touched her Godmother's pendant on her neck and felt a sliver of courage.

"Please, I am begging you. We are all at our wits' end! *Please* explain to us what it will take for you to be a proper fairy! To make some sort of effort. Don't you want that?" her Mother exclaimed, wringing her hands.

The Little Fairy looked at her Mother. Then she looked at her Grand-Mère. Then she realized it was her turn to speak, at last.

"I guess my answer to that is… my answer is maybe I *don't* want to be a proper fairy. At all," she said.

The very idea shocked everyone into another sudden silence.

"You… don't…?" Her Mother couldn't even finish whatever sentence she had begun speaking.

The Little Fairy remembered what her Fairy Godmother had said.

I must be brave, tell them honestly what I desire, and then go find it, she thought.

"I don't want to be a proper fairy because I don't really like living here in the bayou. I want to see the ocean…maybe live there. I don't enjoy flying or dancing…

I enjoy swimming. I *want* to swim. In fact, I want to swim every day, as much as I like. And flower nectar has always made me queasy… I like eating crawfish. And I just don't have any friends here, except old Monsieur Bon Chance. I want to have lots of friends who like the things *I like* and enjoy the things *I enjoy*. I want to BE in a place where I BELONG."

"You want…what?" the Little Fairy's Mother began to speak in a daze.

"Oh, but, we all agree on one thing: I absolutely do *NOT* want to grow up and marry a troll and live in a grotto like Auntie Bluebell."

The Little Fairy's Mother and Grand-Mère's mouths fell open at all of this new and unexpected information.

"She doesn't want…to marry a troll," said her Mother.

"She wants…to eat…crawfish," mumbled her Grand-Mère.

Then, her Grand-Mère burst into laughter.

The Little Fairy and her Mother stared at Grand-Mère as she laughed, louder and louder still, slapping her thighs, and tumbling in the air until she flew onto her backside. And that made her laugh even harder so that tears coursed down her cheeks, and she practically turned purple.

The Little Fairy's Mother began to giggle, then too and that made the Little Fairy also laugh.

"Tee Hee!" her Mother laughed. "Tee hee hee hee haa ha!"

"Hoooo ho ho ho ho!" the Little Fairy's Grand-Mère continued to laugh, lying on her back, now kicking her legs into the air, her wrinkled wings flapping on the leaf floor. Which was a comical sight in itself and caused them all to laugh yet even harder.

"AH HAHAHAHAHAHA!!!!," the Little Fairy's Mother laughed. Her snorting laughter made her fly backwards and upside down.

"HO HO HO HO HO!" they all laughed together. Until they all were laughing and almost crying.

"What's so funny?" asked Sakura and Aster in unison. They had just arrived home from the dance and had no idea what was going on. It was quite a sight after all.

"Ah HAHAHA… your sister… HA HEE hee HEE… your sister said she doesn't… HA HA… she told us she doesn't want to marry a troll!" said her Grand-Mère, still laughing and trying desperately to compose herself, so she could get off the floor.

Sakura and Aster exchanged aghast looks.

"I should think not, that would mean…" began Sakura.

"…that would mean she was going to end up like poor ol' Auntie Bluebell!" finished Aster. The twins often started and finished each other's sentences when they were excited.

At this, the Little Fairy, her Mother and Grand-Mère all laughed anew. Even more than before and even louder.

After a confused moment, Sakura and Aster joined in, just because everyone else was laughing.

Finally, after everyone had a good laugh (which, by the way, works almost as well as a good cry), the Little Fairy fluttered to her Grand-Mère, helped her off the floor, assisted in brushing her off, handed her the *lorgnette* and gave her a big hug and a kiss. Then she fluttered over to her Mother, helped her right herself in the air, and gave her a hug and a kiss as well.

"My Little Fairy," said her Mother, after they had all quieted, clasping her daughter's small rough browned hands in her own soft ones. "Then there is nothing we can say or do to make you want to be a proper fairy?"

The Little Fairy shook her head, *No.*

Her Mother sighed. "Then I guess you must go seek what you want, then."

"Thank you for trying to understand. I think I should leave right away. I have made up my mind to go to the ocean, and it'll be easier if I just go. I think that is where I am supposed to be, where I'll belong," said the Little Fairy.

"Mon Dieu," whispered her Mother. "Must you leave right now, in the dark, in the inky night? How will you fly so far, when you can barely hover?"

Remembering her Godmother had told her to be brave, the Little Fairy replied.

"I suppose I could walk too and maybe even swim a bit."

She looked at her family staring at her and saw with surprise they all looked concerned...and a little sad.

"It could be dangerous," said the Little Fairy's Grand-Mère, gruffly, now that she had recovered from her laughing fit. "You make sure you stay alert and keep your wits about you. Be on the lookout for trolls, pixies, rougarous, highwaymen, and masked shady strangers."

Her Grand-Mère's dire warning made the Little Fairy's resolve waiver – a bit. But she was determined. "I know. But I'm strong and I'm brave," said the Little Fairy. And she touched her necklace again.

"Wait! If you are indeed leaving -," Aster said, looking to Sakura, who nodded as if Aster had given her a silent command, and flitted off to their shared bedroom nook behind a drape of sassafras leaves.

"Then you'd best be equipped for what lies ahead!" Aster finished as Sakura returned in a blink, handing a leaf-wrapped parcel to the Little Fairy.

"What is this?" asked the Little Fairy, taking it and starting to remove the leaf wrapping. And her Mother and Grand-Mère looked equally surprised.

The twins exchanged looks as she began to pull various items out of the parcel. They were various pieces of an outfit, of some sort.

"We wanted to make you something. We were planning on giving it to you anyway - to help protect you whenever you fly, Aster showed me a -" Sakura said.

Aster interrupted "I saw this picture that I found near the levee and it gave me the idea and I showed it to Sakura…"

Sakura continued "…and so I made the jacket, gloves, and helmet out of fig leather and trimmed it in bumblebee fur. Those little boots I made out of fig leather to protect your toes. And I sewed a little waterproof backpack to keep anything you may need to carry or take with you dry and safe. The jacket and backpack should slide perfectly over the base of your wings and…"

Aster added "And I engineered the goggles out of mica flecks. They will help you see better when you're flying and…"

Sakura broke in to finish the thought "…and it'll keep you from poking your eyes out when you fall through the treetops, I mean – er, *IF* you fall through the treetops."

The twins looked at each other, with a knowing look.

"So, try them on!" they both finished, in unison.

Speechless, the Little Fairy donned the wee helmet, jacket, gloves, goggles, protective pads, tiny boots, and backpack.

They fit perfectly and the twin sisters floated about her, admiring the effect.

"NOW you're ready for your journey!" the sisters clapped their hands with glee.

The Little Fairy was so touched by their loving gesture, she couldn't speak.

"You look... very smart," sighed the Little Fairy's Mother, seeing her littlest daughter for the first time in a whole new light.

"It's not necessarily *proper* fairy attire… but it doesn't look half bad," murmured Grand-Mère, nodding begrudgingly, peering at the ensemble through her *lorgnette*.

"Thank you. Thank you all," said the Little Fairy.

"Well. I guess there is nothing left to say except... *Bon chance*," said Sakura, scooping her sibling close and hugging her tight.

"*Au revoir, Sis,*" said Aster once Sakura had released her. Aster bestowed a gentle kiss on her little sister's helmeted brow and adjusted the tiny flight goggles more securely onto her face.

"*Goodbye*," whispered the Little Fairy to them all, her eyes wet with tears that fell and splashed inside her new custom goggles. Leaving was very hard, even though she knew it was the right thing to do.

She turned about, and took off, flying slowly, slowly, very low to the ground, out of her familiar snug fairy home and into the mysterious night, beginning her three-day trip to the sea.

CHAPTER FIVE

THE MASKED STRANGER

Chapter Five:
The Masked Stranger

After flying south all night through the bayou, following the trickling streams in the light of a bright full moon, the Little Fairy made it to a small river. She had grown tired of flying, so she settled into a tree hollow for a quick nap.

When she awoke, she was happy to see a beautiful sunny day had begun.

The river ran merrily through the brush along the banks and all around her, unfamiliar creatures were stirring and starting to enjoy the day. Some of the creatures looked familiar to the Little Fairy, such as a few of the birds and the fish. Even creatures she had never seen before seemed very interesting and appeared quite friendly, including a group of furry creatures that sang a funny spirited song as they ran into and out of the river, taking their morning bath:

"Not a cat, not a rat!

Whiskered, furred,

Sleek and round!

Both of this,

And of that!

In waters of all the world

We are found!

Romp, bevy or raft!

To slide and play is our craft!"

These happy scampering creatures looked as if they were all having the most wonderful time, and it was a joy to watch their antics, but the Little Fairy knew she could not stick around and watch much longer. She had two more full days of travel until she reached her destination, so she readied herself to continue her journey.

"Since I can travel by air OR water, I think I'll swim a little now," the Little Fairy thought. "To the ocean!" she said aloud, touching her Godmother's necklace.

An idea came to her, and she put her flight helmet, goggles and gloves on, but folded her jacket and pants, and placed them and her protective pads and boots into her backpack.

And then she dove into the water.

She dove deep,

deep,

deep,

and deeper still

than any fairy had ever ventured then or since.

Her goggles worked underwater as wonderfully as they had in the air, and they actually helped the Little Fairy to see more clearly. And her flight helmet kept her thick curls dry and her waterproof backpack protected her jacket and boots from the water completely.

Since she was swimming downstream, it was easy to kick her feet and pop up to the surface.

To her delight, she noticed that her wings, when wet, covered her like a wetsuit would, and kept her body mostly dry.

"This is wonderful," she thought happily as she swam with the current, faster and faster. "I wonder what Mother, Grand-Mère, Sakura, Aster, Monsieur Bon Chance and my Godmother would think if they saw me now."

All day, she swam South, not getting tired, and marveling at life in the river and relishing the change in scenery. Water sprites and nymphs playfully splashed at her and called to her to stay and play, but she was determined to make it to the ocean. Fish, swimming alongside and beneath her, shouted encouragement to her. Damselflies and dragonflies swooped with glee past her wet wingtips sticking out of the water, buzzing and singing, *"This way! This way! This way to the Ocean!"*

Every creature seemed to be glad the Little Fairy was on her journey. *"Go on! Go further! Go further!"* they all shouted.

When she grew tired, she managed to float along on her back, somewhat successfully, her wings making an excellent raft.

49

Her round pudginess also helped keep her buoyant, very much like a cork in water.

"These wings do greater good in the water than in air," thought the Little Fairy, bemused.

Traveling this way made time pass quickly and before she could blink, it was soon the beginning of night.

The Little Fairy made her way to a small, dry ledge above the water among the roots of a dark and majestic bald cypress tree. There she flapped her wings dry, took off her helmet, gloves, pads, and goggles, lay them neatly in a row by her side, and fell comfortably asleep atop a makeshift mattress of soft Spanish moss, using her jacket as a blanket.

In the middle of the night, the Little Fairy was jolted awake by an unfamiliar rustling. She sat up, alarmed, remembering her Grand Mère's dire warning of trolls, pixies, rougarous, highwaymen, and masked strangers.

She peeped out around the roots of the cypress to see a large, hunched shape not farther than the length of a human's foot from her. This creature or thing was sitting on a thin sandy ledge along the water, loudly munching on a mulberry.

Quickly and quietly, in case she had to flee from the creature, the Little Fairy put on all of her flight gear again as well as her backpack.

"H-Hello?' she then called out, hesitantly.

The shape whirled about and the Little Fairy emitted a tiny scream, as she could see clearly in the moonlight that the strange creature wore a mask! (Creatures that wore masks must be up to no good, according to fairy etiquette).

"Ah, *Bon Soir*," called out the creature, pleasantly enough. "Would you care for a mulberry? There's plenty." He held out a plump, juicy mulberry in one dark paw.

The Little Fairy was surprised at the kindness in the masked stranger's voice.

"P-proper fairy etiquette says to not trust creatures w-w-with masks," she said, before thinking.

The creature looked mildly offended by her prim response. But he shrugged, and continued eating mulberries, nonplussed.

"Fairy etiquette, eh? Is it proper fairy etiquette to judge someone by appearances? Or to refuse a gift when offered kindly? I'm only offering to share a lovely mulberry from that bush right over there. You look tired and hungry. I'm simply trying to help, *cher*."

The Little Fairy had never considered that.

"You' make a good point. I'm so sorry," she said. And she cautiously fluttered closer to the creature.

"No worries. Apology humbly accepted," replied the creature good-naturedly. He handed her a generous piece of a juicy mulberry, and she took it. Clumsily, she fluttered to a nearby tree stump to eat it, staring at the creature the whole time.

The late meal, the strange appearance of the creature... it was all a bit confusing.

"Besides, this isn't a mask," said the creature, tapping his face. "This is a part of me – I was born this way, see? It's the birthmark of My People. My whole tribe has this same marking on their faces. I sometimes forget it resembles a mask and might make other creatures uncomfortable."

51

"Yes, well, it is pretty scary looking," remarked the Little Fairy, not thinking before she spoke.

She looked up and saw the creature had a quizzical expression on his face.

"Oh, I'm sorry, was that rude?" she asked.

"No, not at all, but I was thinking about that interesting costume you're wearing. Is wearing *that* proper fairy etiquette?"

"Um, no," the Little Fairy said, sheepishly, realizing he had a point. "And truth be told, I've never been really good at following some of the guidelines for proper fairy etiquette," said the Little Fairy.

"Oh yah? Which fairy etiquette guidelines aren't you good at following?" the creature asked.

"Uh, kind of – all of them."

The Little Fairy's bluntly honest answer made the other creature laugh.

"That's why I'm wearing all of this gear." She pointed to her outfit. "I don't fly very well, so these things are supposed to help me on my journey. I'm headed to the ocean. I think I – I think I might belong there."

"Huh," said the creature, who had now finished his midnight snack of mulberries and had ambled to the water's edge. He began to tidily wash his paws, whiskers, and cheeks with the river water. "That so? You think your place is somewhere with the ocean? Well, I think you belong there, too."

"You do?" said the Little Fairy, surprised. "Why would you think that? You just met me."

"Well, because unlike your fairy brethren, I can see you as you really are, inside. Underneath all that getup. I don't see others by what's on the outsides, but by what's in the inside, you see. And you? Your insides show you definitely belong somewhere near the ocean."

The Little Fairy began to grow excited. Forgetting her prior reservations about the Masked Stranger, she leapt up into the air and moved closer towards him, her wings fluttering with excitement. "Really? You can see the REAL ME inside? Tell me about myself then?"

The creature gave her a piercing look and said, "Well now, that's something you're gonna have to find out for yourself, cher. I *could* tell you about the real You, but You probably wouldn't believe me. Besides, I have found that in this life, it's up to each of us to discover our own true Self, instead of being told by others who we really are."

"Oh," said the Little Fairy, crestfallen.

The creature stopped washing his hands and now began drying them by rubbing them briskly together on his furry forearms. He heard her somber tone of voice and paused his fastidious grooming, looking up.

"Ouch. Ok, ok. I can't stand seeing your little sad face, so I tell you what. I'll tell you a riddle to help you a little, ok? And that way the riddle can be like a... kind of like a hint."

The Little Fairy began to get excited again.

"You'll help me? By telling me a riddle? Ok! Yes! Please do! Fairies LOVE riddles."

(This is true. Fairies DO love riddles. And that is in fact, the only part of all of Fairy culture that the Little Fairy had ever enjoyed.)

The creature thought for a moment, then cleared his throat. He next struck a dramatic pose in the moonlight and intoned,

"Ahem. Ok, here goes;

QUATORZE

FOURTEEN

No fairy be

Your destiny

Under moon,

But not raccoon

Not aloft

So not a moth

Nor an owl,

Nor any fowl

Not rabbit and not hare,

Nor a badger, nor a bear.

Third lens within

Big steady bright eyes,

Most curious features

of a most curious creature

of a most curiously modest size

Playful in spirit

Thick skin upon nimble paws,

Lover of water, swimming champ

With these clues,

your riddle is now solved – "

"-Oh, no – uh, hold on a minute, cher-," the creature stopped speaking and paused, paws up, eyes wide, sniffing the air.

"What -," the Little Fairy began.

"Shhhh! Shshshshshshshshhhhhh!" the creature hushed, warning the Little Fairy by waving his paws. He crept closer to her and whispered, "Speak *very* soft. I smell a D-O-G-G-I-Y-E nearby." He sat, still as a stone, eyes darting about, ears perked up.

"Oh," whispered the Little Fairy back, but not understanding why he was acting that way or his poorly spelled out explanation. Dogs never bothered fairies, so the creature's intense concern didn't make much sense to her.

They sat in silence and without moving for what felt like a very long time.

"But what did you mean by 'with all these clues, your riddle is now solved'?" the Little Fairy finally whispered into the Masked Stranger's ear. "I mean my riddle is NOT solved. After all of that, I still don't know the answer. If my destiny is to 'not a fairy be', then what am I?"

The creature stopped standing still and let out a deep relieved breath.

"Okay, I'm truly sorry about that – I - I thought I heard a dog."

"Oooohhh," murmured the Little Fairy, now understanding what he was trying to spell.

"I'll finish the riddle, just 'cause the ending, I think, will really help you - >ahem< - here goes," he said, clearing his throat and once again adopting a dramatic pose, resuming the riddle where he left off.

"-your riddle is now solved!

All these clues, added up, now reveal

the Real You

that has been hidden,

no longer disguised

or concealed:

Not meant to flit and dance in the air

like Fairies,

but join your true tribe

along rivers and ocean's waters.

Your destiny, my Little Fairy,

is to become an – "

But he never got a chance to hear the Little Fairy's guesses as the loud bay of a Catahoula Leopard hound's ***"Aroooooooo!"*** erupted in a booming sound just behind them!

The Little Fairy blinked and in that one second, the Masked Stranger dove headlong into a nearby brush and two short seconds after, a large panting hound bounded into view, rounding the cypress with a speed like a thunderclap and then disappeared into the same brush, in pursuit of the now vanished creature, not even noticing the trembling and shocked Little Fairy.

"Wait! Come back!" cried the Little Fairy. But she already knew it was of no use.

She could hear the pattering steps of the creature running away at a full-on sprint and the pursuing hound's deep ringing cries grow fainter and fainter. She knew from the volume that both creatures were quickly much too far away for her to ever catch up and find out more.

"My destiny is to become an…a… *what*?" the Little Fairy wondered aloud, feeling frustrated and tired.

She washed her hands off in the river, just as the creature had, replaying his words in her head and trying to guess the ending. Then she flapped her wings dry again (she had gotten drenched by a wave of river water, thanks to the hound's energetic chase of the fleeing masked stranger).

Returning to her makeshift bed in the Spanish moss, the Little Fairy repeated the last words of the riddle over and over again, still sleepily trying to puzzle it out. "Your destiny is to become an... Your destiny is to become a... Your... destiny... is...to... to... Zzzzzzzzz.""

The answer never came.

The day's excitement had taken its toll: the Little Fairy fell into a deep, dreamless sleep, while still mouthing the riddle's strange last words.

CHAPTER SIX

~ LIGHT GREEN WINGS ~

5

AT LONG LAST, SHE ARRIVES!

UNDERNEATH SOUTHERN SKIES

5

NIGHT'S SYMBOL OF BEGINNINGS

AN UNEXPECTED AND UNWELCOME
DEVELOPMENT

Chapter Six:
An Unexpected and Unwelcome Development

The next morning, the Little Fairy awoke to another sunny day and was surprised to see how big the river was now.

Her encounter with the masked creature and his odd riddle from the night before was quickly forgotten and she regarded the river with glee.

"The river is much bigger, and the water is going faster," she said. "This must mean… I am near the ocean!"

And she leapt about in sheer happiness!

Quickly, she tried to flutter her wings to fly into the air, but something seemed odd with her wings. They somehow seemed glued to her body!

"But…what is this? They should not be! I thought I shook them completely dry last night! Oh NO!" She cried. "What has happened to me?"

She tried, unsuccessfully, to pry her wings away from her body, but they seemed stuck fast to her back. Worse still, she felt along her arms and feet and realized that instead of just her wings being furry, she was now entirely covered in fur! Her arms, her face, everything! Covered in thick, dense fur!!! And –lo! She even had whiskers on her face! Actual long twitchy whiskers!!!

And… wait a minute… what was that… could that be a…? …protruding from…?

"Alors!" she screamed. "What evil witchcraft is this???"

"I HAVE A TAIL!???!!"

"Oh Mon Dieu, Mon Dieu!" She shrieked in anguish. "I have been stricken with some awful river-whisker-fur-and-tail growing disease! Oh! Oh! Oh! And I can never return home like this!"

Not knowing what else to do, she began to cry.

"Oh! I should have just stayed where I was and tried harder to be a proper fairy! At least I would not be this… furry…monster…thing," she sobbed.

"Why are you crying, dear child?" asked a familiar voice.

The Little Fairy opened her eyes to see her Fairy Godmother, the Silver Fairy, hovering in front of her.

"Yes. I am here. Now why are you crying?" asked the Silver Fairy.

"Loo- look at m-m-m-e Fairy Godmother," she gulped. "I have turned into a m-m-monster!"

The Silver Fairy gasped.

"No, dear! You are not monstrous! Not in any way! You are quite a beautiful creature! You have changed most wonderfully! You are now most exquisitely suited for your new life!"

The Little Fairy (who no longer even remotely resembled a fairy) was shocked by her Fairy Godmother's cheerful remarks.

"But- but do you not see all of this? My face… my arms… my hands… aighh!! What happened to my hands!" she screamed suddenly.

(Because, you see, there was now webbing between the fingers of her hands and yes, her toes too. She hadn't noticed it until just that moment.)

"And… And…," the Little Fairy looked about, "Oh! And worse still, I seem to also become a giant! Just LOOK at this, Godmother!" she held out her wee flight helmet, goggles, tiny gloves, protective pads, and jacket. They all looked incredibly tiny as they now all fit in the palm of just one of her furred, transformed hands.

Her tears fell fast and thick from her eyes as she regarded the tiny flight gear she had so recently worn. "I've just grown so HUGE! I couldn't possibly use these ever again!!!"

The Silver Fairy smiled in satisfaction. "Ah yes! That's right! Exactly!"

"Ohhh! What will I do??? Looking like this, I can nev-never go back to being a fai-fai-fairyyyyy," she wailed.

The Silver Fairy said nothing, she just pursed her lips and looked at the Little Fairy intently.

The Little Fairy – er, I mean, you know who – just kept sobbing. And sobbing. And sobbing.

Soon the grass around her and her furry feet – er- or rather her paws - were quite soaked.

But she finally did stop sobbing.

And when she stopped and wiped her eyes, she saw the Silver Fairy calmly looking at her.

And then the Silver Fairy spoke.

"Past that last bend in the river is the ocean," she said, softly.

She pointed in the distance and there, only a bit further, was a glittering line, shining and sparkling in the sun.

"You are too close to go back now. Don't you remember what you told me you wanted?" she asked, her wee wings whir-whirring in the air.

The Little Fairy quieted and wiped off her face with her paws.

"Don't you remember?"

"Yyyy-y-yes," she said, with a sniffle.

"Then go, my dear. Embrace the rest of the adventure. Disregard what you think you *should* look like or *should* be. Because, as you know, all great adventurers share one very important trait: ***they never turn back***."

Wiping her face some more, the Little Fairy began to really open her eyes and started to ask –

-but then said nothing.

Because the Silver Fairy had once again vanished into the air.

CHAPTER SEVEN

ONZE

I AM
EVERYTHING, CREATION HOLLOWED OUT
I STEAL YOUR VOICE AWAY
BUT THEN RETURN IT
WHISPER TO WHISPER
      SHOUT TO SHOUT

Chapter Seven:
The Little Fairy's Destiny

"Well at least I can still swim," The Little Fairy said to herself as she dove into the cool water.

Indeed, her new features helped her swim even better. Her webbed paws paddled and pulled her through the water with ease. Her slick fur covered body kept her buoyant by trapping air around her. And her tail guided her easily through the river by undulating in a smooth left to right motion, helping her maintain a straight course on the river, very much like how a boat rudder helps to steer a boat.

With each skillful stroke of her paws, she became more at ease and more coordinated. She began to swim faster and faster, slicing through the water like an arrow.

"Hmph," she said to herself. "I seem to be swimming faster than ever. I do believe I will reach the ocean in only another hour or so… but oh wait …there it is! I'm passing the last bend in the river!"

Before her lay the last piece of disappearing bank and after that… like the end of the earth… was the sea.

With delight, with happiness, she forgot her odd new appearance and sadness at no longer being a fairy and she swam faster than ever towards the ever-widening horizon of the big, beautiful sea.

All around her – at long last - she could see nothing the blue breaking waves of water and the riverbanks stretching into long beaches of sand.

"I'm here!" she cried. She splashed and dove deep with delight.

"I'm here!" she called out to a swimming school of small fish, and they all politely cheered for her, shouting underwater; "Yaybbblaaayyybblubbleyyyy!" (Well, that *is* what "Yay" sounds like underwater!)

"I'm here!" she laughed, and she swam celebratory underwater backward loop-de-loops, just as her sisters, Sakura and Aster had in the air.

"At last! At last! Look! HERE is La Mer! Look! It is just as Monsieur Bon Chance described! I am finally in the ocean!!!" And she dove and spun and flipped and leapt as she never had before when she had wings. She was as naturally elegant in the water as she had been awkward and fumbling in the air.

Once she had swum to her heart's content and calmed down, she lay on her back, floating, feeling excited and happy, and she looked up peacefully into the bright blue sky.

"That's a nice bit of swimming, there," said an admiring voice from somewhere behind and to her left.

The Little Fairy started with fright and turned about to see several creatures in the water, not too far away from her, staring at her in awe.

They too were relaxing by floating on their backs in the water and enjoying what looked like a fine breakfast in the sun. Several of them had crayfish in their paws, which they crunched with relish.

One of them cheerfully gestured to her, waving a half-eaten crayfish. "What I meant to say, was, where did you learn how to swim like that?" And the creature grinned at her and wiped the back of his mouth with his paw.

The Little Fairy suddenly felt self-conscious, remembering how odd she now looked.

"I-I-I taught myself how."

"Henri, you are being rude," complained another creature. "Here she is, a lovely new river otter just arrived, and you start right off with pestering her about her swim technique."

"*Otter?*" said the Little Fairy, confused.

"Yes, dear," said the same creature, who seemed, in manner and mien, to be the oldest in the group. In fact, something about her authoritative air and sharp reprimand to the young Henri reminded the Little Fairy of her Grand Mère.

"I'm sorry," the creature continued. "Please excuse our rudeness and the rudeness of my youngest son, Henri. He was quite impressed with your diving, you see, and he is always so very curious."

The Little Fairy had an odd sensation, then, of recognition. She looked down at her own hands –er-paws and then at the group before her. They all had the same paws.

She looked at the fur covering her body.

They all had the same type of fur… some were grayer or more dark warm brown or more sandy tan or whitish grey, but they all had the same…

She felt along her face and touched her long, twitchy whiskers.

They all had long, twitchy whiskers.

She looked back at her tail and then looked at theirs… and she gasped!

The puzzle pieces of who the Little Fairy really was now seemed to click into place; why she always felt at home in the water but uncomfortable in the air, the urge to stay with the unfamiliar yet playful group of furry creatures she had spotted on her journey, and the last missing word of the unfinished riddle the masked creature had shared with her; "

And she finally, *finally* understood.

"*Mon Dieu!* I am not a little fairy anymore*!* I have become what I was always meant to be!

I have become an *otter*!"

CHAPTER EIGHT

I AM
THE MIDDLE OF A HURRICANE
BUT NOT SPELLED THE SAME

I AM THE MIDDLE OF EVERY ENDING THE BEGINING OF IN THE BEGINING

ONE LETTER AM I. ALSO A NUMBER OF THE SHORTEST WORDS EVER HEARD

I AM ALSO YOU
WHEN JUST I LETTER
IS YOUR NAME.

EIGHT   HUIT

A PLACE IN THIS WORLD

Chapter Eight:
A Place in This World

From a distant shore, the Silver Fairy saw the river otters heartily welcome the new river otter that once upon a time used to be the unhappy Little Fairy, into their tribe. Satisfied that all was well, she turned about to flit back to the bayou.

Before she left, however, she spied something glinting in the rays of the early sun.

Bending down, she plucked a tiny silver necklace from the sand upon which hung a silver and blue stone. In the early morning light, the stone's surface seemed to ripple like tiny waves.

Smiling knowingly, the Silver Fairy stuck the necklace in one of her many teeny tiny pockets and flew off into the sky, humming a happy tune, making whirling delighted curlicues in the air.

Later, she would visit the family of the Little Fairy Who Was No Longer A Fairy, and they would be delighted to hear the report that the Little Fairy had finally found her true heart's desire and her place in the world.

As for Monsieur Bon Chance, you can imagine his happiness once he heard of the good fortune of his little friend, who used to be so sad and uncomfortable in the bayou... like the proverbial fish out of water.

It is probably safe to assume that once he heard of her fate, he chuckled and gleefully blew bubbles, all the while chomping on a stolen meal of pink marshmallows.

And so, this is where the adventure ends of the former Little Bayou Fairy.

BUT WAIT... here is a quick postscript –

Should you ever visit the Louisiana coast, sometime in the spring, a few miles away from Grande Isle, I bet you will see our little heroine in real life… for you see, The Little Bayou Fairy Who is No Longer A Fairy lives there, to this very day.

Watch for her in the Springtime when the sun is out and the crayfish are plenty… chances are she will be near the shore, playing with her fish friends and her otter family. Or you may find her bobbing further out in the ocean, teasing the dolphins, paddling past the sea turtles, or having long, philosophical conversations with the noble sperm whales.

…And since there is no happier otter in the world than that particular otter, I know you will recognize her at once.

C'est ainsi, n'est pas? (It is so, is it not?)

SEIZE

SIXTEEN

Thank you, gentle reader, for following this quirky fairy tale.

Here we will take leave of our once little fairy and in her new life, wish her well.

Everything concluded, rest assured,

Exactly as it was meant to be.

Not perhaps the way the fairy had planned, but a perfect ending, nonetheless, befitting her true

Destiny.

Deux

ERASE THE START OF REGRET
CUT SHORT AND REASSEMBLE GREETINGS
ONCE CORRECT, THE WHITE BIRD YOU SEEK
WILL FINALLY APPEAR!

Glossary of Louisiana and Patois Terms in this Book

Louisiana has many influences from many different points on the globe; France, Britain, Spain, Germany, Poland, Vietnam, First Nations like the Chitimacha and Choctaw, Free and Enslaved People of Color, and Nova Scotia have all had an influence on the language, customs, foods, and folklore of the state's inhabitants. Many of the terms in this book come from my own family who reside in Louisiana, a language of our ancestors called Creole Patois (CREE-ol PAH-twah) that originated from France. I've tried to spell out the words the way we say them phonetically. If it looks French but doesn't sound French the way I spelled it phonetically, that's because it has evolved into its own localized flavor. Enjoy! Or as we say in Louisiana ""Laissez fait les bon temp roulez!" (Let the Good Times Roll)!

Adieu: Pron. "AH-dew" Meaning: "Bye"

Alors: Pron. "AH-lors" Meaning: "Oh no!" Old fashioned. No longer really in use. Equivalent to "darn".

Atchafalalaya: Pron. "At CHA Fa Laya" Chitimacha origin meaning "Long River". The beautiful wild setting for this story and where almost all of the storyline takes place. The largest wetland and swamp in the United States. Also, as of this printing, is an endangered environment. To find out more about the important role the Atchafalaya Basin plays in the health of our environment, please check out an important non profit that has undertaken the task of restoring and preserving this very truly magical place: www.basinkeeper.org

Au Revoir: Pron. "OHV-wahr" Meaning: Good Bye (More formal)

Bon Chance: Pron. "BAHN chans" Meaning: Good Luck!

Changeling: Legends vary, but the term is English and means more or less a child replaced with another, usually without the mother knowing. Sometimes the child is changed out with another species' child altogether. Humans talk of changelings being orchestrated by fairies but fairies also have their own myths about other creatures swapping their babies, too.

C'est ainsi: Pron. "SAY ahnsay" Meaning: "It is so." More commonly said as "Oui, C'est Ainsi." "WEE, SAY ahnsay" (Yes, it is so)

Fee or Fifolet: Pron. "FEE foh lay" Meaning: Louisiana Fairies. Traditionally seen as bad omens, they usually appeared as glowing balls of blue light. If you followed one into a swamp, you were doomed as you were certain to become hopelessly lost. Fortunately, no creepy mean fairies misleading any wayward travelers in this tale!

Formidable: Pron. "FOR mee dahblah" Meaning: "Wonderful"

Grand-mère: Pron. "GRAND Mahr" Meaning: "Grandmother"

Jean Lafitte: Although not specifically mentioned in this book, I would encourage (hint hint) readers to research this infamous profiteer. His route through the swamps and waterways of Louisiana to evade the law with ill-gotten gains has inspired many legends and myths and rumor has it that there is still treasure to be found along the coast and throughout the Basin itself.

Lagniappe:

La Mer: Pron: "LA Maher" Meaning: The sea

Mais: Pron. "MAY" Meaning: "But!" Slang. An exclamation of disbelief.

Mais Non: Pron. "MAY NO!" Meaning: "But no!" Slang. An exclamation of extreme disbelief.

Mon Dieu: Pron. "Mon DEHW" Meaning: "My God!" or "My Goodness!" A declaration of distress or amazement.

Monsieur: Pron. "MISS you" Meaning: "Good sir", formal address, like how we say "Mr. or Mrs."

N'est pas: Pron. "Nays PA" Meaning: "Is it not?"

Petite: Pron. "PEE-TEE" Meaning: Little.

Pirogue: Pron. "PEER-oh" Meaning: A long narrow flat bottom boat, ideal for navigating the shallow waters of the swamp.

Pince Nez: Pron. "PAHNS Nay" Meaning: Glasses that do not have earpieces attached. Name originates from French "Pincer" to pinch and "Nez" nose.

Rougarou: Pron. "ROO gar OO" Meaning: A Creole Werewolf. Also called a Loup-Garou.

Que: Pron. "Kay" Meaning: What. Can be used as part of a sentence or general exclamation.

Sacré bleu: Pron. "Sah Kra BLEW". Meaning: Expression of amazement, surprise, dismay, or exasperation.

And finally,

FIN (The End)

Excerpts from
"Daisy Nettlebee's Fairy Etiquette Compendium"
(The Ultimate Guide to Fairy Manners, Mores,
Merrymaking, and Mayhem)
By Dame Daisy Nettlebee, ROFE
(Royal Order of the Fairy Empire)

From Chapter 12 "Nectar Consumption and Acceptable Levels of Indulgence", pages 33-37:

"When proffered nectar, accept your leaf cup with gracious gaiety. Once leaf cup is in hand, sip, never slurp OR burp. Enjoy nectar moderately as everyone knows greedy fairies make terrible friends and inelegant dance partners. It is the essence of good breeding to display quiet enthusiasm, tact, and grace upon being offered such delectable floral refreshment."

"Heed the sad tale of Marigold Flint, who, during one fateful night, ingested too much bluebonnet nectar, tumbled from the air into a tiny human's open lunchbox and fell into a deep slumber atop a bag of crunchy fish-shaped crackers. The next morning, the human owner of the lunchbox appeared without warning and snapped the lunchbox shut, not bothering to look inside, and then hurried off to board a great yellow contraption called a "bus". Later that day, the tiny human returned within the same yellow contraption as he usually did. But what of poor Marigold? It saddens me to report that she was never seen nor heard from again. Rumor has it she met her demise in a malevolent land called "kindergarten" that has horrifying numbers of tiny, excited humans, most likely during torturous ritual tiny humans excitedly describe as "Show and Tell."

"If one finds oneself in the unfortunate circumstance of having ingested more nectar than one is accustomed, it is best to remain sheltered in the nearest leaf nook or flower bower until the effects have abated. NEVER overindulge in nectar and try to fly home!"

From Chapter 18 "Associations with Beings Other Than Fairies", pages 65- 72:

"Do not play with possums. They will try to eat you."

"Do not frolic with foxes. They will try to eat you."

"Do not associate with alligators. They will try to eat you."

"Do not natter with nutria. They will try to eat you."

"Do not banter with bears. They will try to eat you."

"Do not chatter with cranes. They will try to eat you."

"Do not scamper with snakes. They will try to eat you."

"Do not chat with cows. They will try to eat you."

"Do not tamper with turtles. They will try to eat you."

"Do not talk with toads. They will try to eat you."

"Do not lounge with lizards. They will try to eat you."

"Do not palaver with polecats. You will stink forever, and they will also try to eat you."

"Do not conversate with cats. They won't just try to eat you— they CAN and WILL eat you."

"Do not investigate or go near anything other than the creatures listed on the approved short list (see next page) as acceptable, because fairy statistics have proven time and time again, whatever creatures you might encounter in the world that are bigger than an average fairy WILL TRY TO EAT YOU."

"Most human beings should be avoided. A fairy should be particularly wary of immature humans called "infants", as these tiniest of humans are prone to careless, wing-crushing, grabbing and will put anything in their mouths. Nine times out of ten, an infant will try and ingest any fairy careless enough to be found within their little arm's reach. (RIP Snowdrop Riverwillow). The exceptions to this practice are human children who are either 4 to 12 years of age or children's book authors, as these two particular human subsets are often found to be atypically kind and friendly towards fairies."

"Fairies should avoid water and water-dwelling creatures at all costs as no good has ever come of such associations."

"Do not make acquaintance with a unicorn – not because it will try and eat you, but a unicorn WILL DEFINITELY INGEST anything and everything else, then loiter about, leaving appallingly large and unsanitary mounds of glitter droppings. Do not let a unicorn's rainbow-hued flowy mane and tail, adorably innocent doe eyes, delicate appearance, and heavenly scent of hopes and dreams overtake your sensibilities. Many an unwise fairy has been eaten out of leaf house and home by the smallest and most beguiling of unicorns."

"The following is the official approved short list of creatures outside of one's tribe with whom a proper fairy may choose to associate;

1. *Birds*
2. *Butterflies, Damselflies, and Dragonflies*
3. *Bees*
4. *Mice, Shrews, Voles, and Moles*
5. *Rabbits*
6. *Dogs*
7. *Chipmunks, Hedgehogs, and Squirrels*
8. *Deer*
9. *Human children aged 4 -12 and Children's Book Authors*
10. *The occasional orb spider that can spell*
11. *Renaissance Faire attendees*

Any other creatures beyond this list are suspect and probably dangerous. It is also HIGHLY advisable to avoid any creature wearing a mask. The one notable exception for mask wearers are human beings as they often wear masks to prudently prevent and curtail disease transmissions.

It should also be noted that there is rarely such a thing as a good troll. Best to avoid them completely."

From Chapter 20 "Word play, Riddles, and Matches of Wit", pages 99-101

One of the most revered and accepted activities of fairies is word play, cryptographs, riddles, acrostics, and matches of wit. There is a rumor that Alberti's disk was inspired by a tinier version found during a stroll that undoubtedly was fairy-made. (Please see littlebayourfairy.com to read more about this amazing device, used for coded messages! STRONG HINT: There also may be a riddle or two there that uses the disc that MIGHT be needed for the treasure hunt mentioned in the Fairy Godmother's letter! Many times, fairies will place a wager or prize to be won during matches of intellect, code breaking, and bouts of riddle telling. This is an ancient practice that fairies use to keep their wits sharp and to oftentimes fool humans into giving up precious cargo (Rumpelstiltskin, anyone?)

Acrostics in particular are a classic fairy favorite, and the Louisiana fairies are no exception as here is one specific to the region where they live:

ONE

Just four letters form
A distinctive New Orleans style melody
Zig-gle notes here
Zag-gle notesthere
Join us all together and sweet music fills the air!

Here's a riddle that Louisiana fairies love and it's actually not one they coined, but one a human coined long ago that the fairies "borrowed":

TWELVE

"Reeds that product honey without bees"

Here is a "Stabilus" for part of an Alberti's desk designed by the Little Bayou Fairy's sisters, Aster and Sakura. In fact, they cheekily used parts of their names as the key.

Hmmm.... There are two parts to every Alberti's disk cypher. Where then is the "Mobilus"...? Can you think of where that might be?

Again, please refer to www.littlebayoufairy.com for more about cryptography, riddles, acrostics and codes.

*And look sharp as there **MAY** be (strong hint) a crucial piece of information needed for the treasure hunt located there.*

From Chapter 25 "Best Practices of Excellent Fairy Aviators and Choreographers", pages 112-127:

"Fairy flight should always be (as the ancient sayings go)
Light as a feather/
With effortless care/
As graceful and weightless/
As petals on air."

"Do not attempt to ride on the back of another winged creature when one's wings are perfectly functional., It is considered lazy and impolite to do so."

"Fairy wings should be maintained fastidiously
with mindful grooming and constant inspection.
Allowing small tears and threadbare spots on one's wings to accumulate
not only is unsafe for flight but demonstrates shameful dereliction."

"When gathering with other fairies,
proper form is to frolic, fly, and dance/
from sundown to sunup to sundown again,
or any moment you have a chance."

"No fairy dance is enhanced
by dour expressions
sulky gestures
and mood dampening ennui."

An Important Letter From
The Fairy Godmother to Aunt Bluebell
(aka Treasure Hunt Information)

Dear Little Humans:

The letter on the following pages was shared with me by the Little Fairy's Aunt Bluebell (you recall that she eloped to Vegas with a troll and then moved into a slimy grotto as a starterhome?)

Well, this letter is extremely important to share with you because it reveals that The Little Fairy's pendant given to her by her Fairy Godmother has been magically hidden – in REAL LIFE! So you or any child – especially a human child – can locate it, using this book and the Little Bayou Fairy website.

I made sure to include the letter here for you, dear reader, in the hopes that you or one of the little human readers of this tale will be able to decipher the numerous cyphers and riddles and find the hidden pendant.

If you are under 12 years old, you have a good chance at becoming the next owner of the magical silver pendant that the Silver Fairy aka The Fairy Godmother gave to The Little Fairy in the story.

For more details, please refer to **www. littlebayoufairy.com**

PLEASE NOTE (AND THIS IS CRITICALLY IMPORTANT) THAT THE REAL PENDANT IS <u>NOT BURIED ANYWHERE PHYSICALLY!</u> IT IS HIDDEN AWAY SAFELY IN THE FAIRY REALM SO DO NOT GO RUNNING ABOUT DIGGING UP PEOPLE'S LAWNS! Read the letter find out how to hopefully attain the treasure!

Good hunting and Good Fortune! - E.R.B.

"Dearest Bluebell,

I cannot tell you how sad I've felt upon learning of attempts made to steal your niece's talisman, the magical silver pendant I gave her, that helped inspire her to seek her Destiny. You knew very well (*as all we wee folk do*) that Trolls covet treasure, especially silver. And it grieves me that your husband's Troll relations (even though they were distant, and four times removed) were the ones who dared try and abscond it. It was quite foolish of you to let the Troll's gift of flower nectar loosen your tongue about the unique value of the pendant. Of course they would try to find and take it. Luckily, our Little Fairy no longer needs the pendant to find her way. And being wise, I have a plan to get the pendent to its next rightful owner and have a bit of fun in the process. What's life without a bit of fun?

We are so fortunate that the jewel smith who fashioned the talisman, Madame Pixie Dillsaver, placed a most powerful charm upon it-the famous *Pixie Puzzle Protection Proven to Prevent Purloining* TM (Patent Pending) – just in case *anyone* or *anything* dared try to steal it.

The pendant has vanished and relocated it itself to a safe place, as a security measure, to remain out of thieving hands. It will remain vanished until a human or fairy child, one of an age no older than 12 human years, solves the 17 riddles, hidden within this illustrated manuscript and, it is rumored, also on the website www.littlebayoufairy.com.

To help guide young questors to the verity of the riddles and codes, I have placed my seal, the light grey *fleur-de-lis* near each genuine clue. Human children should consult the Glossary to understand what a fleur-de-lis looks like.

"But I only spy 16 fleurs-de-lis total!" I can almost hear you complaining already, Bluebell.

(And I know that is what you are thinking, because I am, after all, a Fairy Godmother!)

You are correct. There ARE only 16 riddles in plain sight. However, the 17th - and final - riddle is made by assembling all of the answers of the original 16!

Once the 17th riddle is assembled AND solved, then the human child may send their answer to this email: *erica@LittleBayouFairy.com.*

Also be aware that if you find yourself MISSING any answers, refer to the "riddles" section on the Little Bayou Fairy website. You MIGHT find some help there!

Alas, there IS a time limit for a child to recover the pendant. The charm stops working on 06-24-2022 (known as International Fairy Day in the human world) at midnight, EST.

After that moment, no more guesses are allowed AND the puzzle portal shall shut and remain shut.

But, I have high hopes that many clever children will winnow out the correct answer and submit their guess, so at 9 am EST the following day (6-25-22) I shall send a message to the parents of the child determined by Fairy Council to have submitted the correct and most true answer, via ePost, to share with them the happy news. The pendant shall then be delivered safely and securely, protected against all magical n'er do wells, into the hands of the chosen child.

I know that this can be very confusing indeed to humans who are not often exposed to the ways and foibles of magic, I have asked my friend, that loquacious but good-hearted scribe Mrs. Ramsey-Bowen, to share these parameters with further detail and with simpler, more human-like clarity on her eWebpage: *www.LittleBayouFairy.com.*

Human parents and children may safely navigate this webpage for more details on rules and even some updates on clues, games and Little Fairy activities, etc.

So, Bluebell, in short, do not exert further energy to seeking the pendant or pleading for its return. You had your chance to guard it and this is the result. You will not find it. You (nor anyone else) won't be able to dig it up, stumble across it, or even divine its location via magic. That would be as much of a fool's errand as those of the pitiful fortune seekers who continue to hunt for the fabled Gentleman Pirate's riches within these swamplands.

The pendant's fate now lies only in the hands and powers of observation and deduction of a wonderful child.

I must admit the thought makes me glad. I wish every child success who dares tackle this quest. It won't be easy, but hopefully entertaining. *(I do find that sometimes the journey yields more fulfillment than arriving at the final destination, don't you?)*

At any rate, regards to you and that Troll husband of yours, Bluebell.

As for your husband, Edgar, rest assured I do not think ill of him, despite everything, - he is not to be held at fault for the churlish actions of his distant Troll cousins because

"-as that solemn saying goes:
one cannot ever pick one's relatives.
but with nimble fingers,
and clear resolve
one can always manage
to pick one's nose."

Whimsically and Long-Windedly Yours,

~The Silver Fairy

PS – See next page to see what humans call a "photograph" of the pendant as a visual reference:

THE MAGICAL PENDANT IS REAL!!!
Go to www.littlebayoufairy.com to find out
more details about the treasure hunt!

Although hidden in the fairy realm, the pendant is indeed real. Designed by the author and fashioned by Atlanta jeweler Tasha Dillsaver, the custom pendant is made of silver, decorated by hand with enamel, and set with an orange garnet. A very special private message for its wearer is engraved on the back. The author was inspired by her favorite childhood illustrator/author, Kit Williams, whose beautifully illustrated treasure hunting book, "Masquerade" gave her endless hours of fun puzzle solving. Thank you (belatedly), Kit!

(Author photo courtesy of Kevin Harry, Photographer)

ABOUT THE AUTHOR AND ILLUSTRATOR, ERICA RAMSEY-BOWEN

Although she has illustrated children's books for many wonderful authors, this is Erica Ramsey-Bowen's first written *AND* illustrated book. Erica resides in Atlanta with her long-suffering husband, Scott, and their opinionated little Maltie dog, Boomer.

Her next fictional children's book in the works is *Free Unicorn*, scheduled to be published sometime on or around Christmas of 2022.

Erica is also working on a four part non-fiction graphic novel based on her real correspondence with noted WWI historians in search of the true gender of the famed pigeon, Cher Ami during the COVID pandemic and civil unrest in America in 2020.

She readily admits the research needed for this project is daunting, but she is delusional enough to believe she is up to the task.

You can follow Erica Ramsey-Bowen on Instagram and Twitter at: Cre8WhatYouWish or on Facebook at: The Little Bayou Fairy.

Erica is pleased to share that a portion of every book sale is being donated to Atchafalaya Basinkeeper, a wonderful organization doing amazing things to restore and preserve the real-life Magical realm that is the Atchafalaya Basin. You can find out more about them by going to: *www.basinkeeper.org.*

Thank You for Your support!!